Merry-Go

A BRISA STORY

By Sibley Miller

Illustrated by Tara Larsen Chang and Jo Gershman

Feiwel and Friends

For Nathaniel—Sibley Miller

For my daughter, Kailin, who has been my most frequent
companion to the County Fair . . .
—Tara Larsen Chang

For the lovely horses of Roze-El Stables, who are always
willing to pose for the price of a carrot.
—Jo Gershman

A FEIWEL AND FRIENDS BOOK
An Imprint of Macmillan

WIND DANCERS: MERRY-GO-HORSES. Copyright © 2011
by Reeves International, Inc. All rights reserved. Distributed in Canada
by H.B. Fenn and Company Ltd.
BREYER, WIND DANCERS, and BREYER logos are trademarks and/or
registered trademarks of Reeves International, Inc. Printed in March
2011 in China by Leo Paper, Heshan City, Guangdong Province. For
information, address Feiwel and Friends, 175 Fifth Avenue,
New York, N.Y. 10010.

Library of Congress Cataloging-in-Publication Data

Miller, Sibley.
Merry go horses : a Brisa story / by Sibley Miller ; illustrated by
Tara Larsen Chang and Jo Gershman. — 1st ed.
p. cm. — (Wind Dancers ; #10)
Summary: The tiny Wind Dancers are so enchanted by the county fair,
from the jumping show horses to the carousel rides, that they
do not want to return home.
ISBN: 978-0-312-60543-8 (alk. paper)
[1. Horses—Fiction. 2. Magic—Fiction. 3. Fairs—Fiction.]
I. Chang, Tara Larsen, ill. II. Gershman, Jo, ill. III. Title.
PZ7.M63373Mer 2011   [E]—dc22
2010014912

Series editor: Susan Bishansky
Design by Barbara Grzeslo
Feiwel and Friends logo designed by Filomena Tuosto

First Edition: 2011

1   3   5   7   9   10   8   6   4   2

www.feiwelandfriends.com

CONTENTS

Meet the Wind Dancers

One day, a lonely little girl named Leanna blows on a doozy of a dandelion. To her delight and surprise, four tiny horses spring from the puff of the dandelion seeds!

Four tiny horses with shiny manes and shimmery wings. Four magical horses who can fly!

Dancing on the wind, surrounded by magic halos, they are the Wind Dancers.

The leader of the quartet is Kona. She has a violet-black coat and vivid purple mane, and she flies inside a halo of magical flowers.

Brisa is as pretty as a tropical sunset with her coral-pink color and blonde mane and tail. Magical jewels make up Brisa's halo, and she likes to admire her gems (and herself) every time she looks in a mirror.

Sumatra is silvery blue with sea-green wings. Much like the ocean, she can shift from calm to stormy in a hurry. Her magical halo is made up of ribbons, which flutter and dance as she flies.

The fourth Wind Dancer is—surprise!—a colt. His name is Sirocco. He's a fiery gold, and he likes to go-go-go. Everywhere he goes, his magical halo of butterflies goes, too.

The tiny flying horses live together in the dandelion meadow in a lovely house carved out of the trunk of an apple tree. Every day, Leanna wishes she'll see the magical little horses again. (She's sure they're nearby, but she doesn't know they're invisible to people.) And the Wind Dancers get ready for their next adventure.

CHAPTER 1
Drive-by Brisa

One sparkling morning, high above their dandelion meadow, the four brightly colored Wind Dancers took flight.

Kona pranced on the air.

Sumatra zipped along.

Sirocco somersaulted from one cloud to the next.

And Brisa, as usual, bobbed on the breeze. Every now and then, she twirled around to admire the curls of her blonde mane and the sparkle of her magic jewels.

"I'm *starving*!" Sirocco neighed, as the

butterflies in his magic halo nodded in agreement.

"You're *always* hungry, Sirocco," Brisa burbled. "Even if we'd just *had* a huge breakfast, you'd be hungry!"

 "But we *didn't* just eat a huge breakfast," Sirocco pointed out.

"It's true," Sumatra agreed. "We didn't have any breakfast today!"

Kona put a hoof on her own belly, trying to quiet its rumbling.

"If we all focus on flying instead of on being hungry," she said evenly, "we'll make it to Leanna's garden and get breakfast."

"Carrots!" Brisa cooed.

"The ones in Leanna's garden *are* super-big," Sirocco replied. "Just one can feed all of us *and* leave enough leftovers for a carrot pudding!"

"As if you're *ever* hungry right after a meal, Sirocco," Sumatra teased.

"Speaking of our favorite girl, Leanna," Brisa said, "I wonder what she's doing today."

"Maybe Leanna and her dog will go to the big horses' paddock to visit the doggies!" Kona suggested, her eyes lighting up at the thought of the puppy who had lived with them before finding his way back to his canine family in the paddock.

"Or maybe . . ." Brisa said, as the Wind Dancers arrived at Leanna's farm house, "she'll just get into a truck and go away."

Her friends looked at her quizzically.

"That's not a very fun thought, is it?" Kona replied.

Brisa cocked her head.

"Maybe not," she said. "But look!"

Kona, Sirocco, and Sumatra followed the pink filly's gaze and gasped. Leanna was indeed tromping toward her family's red pickup truck. Her parents and her little sister, Sara, were with her. And each of them was weighed down with stuff.

Leanna carried an open cardboard box with the biggest, most beautiful tomato Brisa had ever seen.

Sara had two pretty painted model horses in her arms.

The girls' mother toted a large flowerpot brimming with pink roses.

And their dad lugged a picnic cooler and a jug of lemonade.

The family packed everything in their truck.

"We better get going!" Leanna said to her family as the Wind Dancers hovered invisibly nearby. "My tomato has to be in place for judging before ten!"

"Why would anyone judge a tomato?" Sirocco asked. "Did it commit a crime?"

While the colt laughed at his own joke, Sumatra rolled her eyes.

"I wonder where they're going?" she mused.

"Wherever it is, it's too bad for us," Kona said, with a whinny. "I was looking forward to a little Leanna time today. Oh well, what do you horses want to do instead?"

"Wind sprints?" Sirocco proposed.

"Dance practice?" Sumatra offered.

Her eyes still fixed on Leanna's family, Kona asked, "And Brisa? What's your vote?"

When Brisa didn't answer, Kona looked around.

"Brisa?"

"Where did she disappear to?" the violet filly asked Sumatra and Sirocco.

Sumatra looked around for a moment, too. Then her eyes went wide.

"Look!" she gasped.

She pointed her nose toward the pickup truck. There, perched on Leanna's big shiny tomato was . . . Brisa!

"Come along, Brisa!" Sirocco called. "Our carrot awaits!"

But Brisa was so busy settling onto Leanna's smooth, fleshy tomato, sniffing its earthy aroma, and admiring its beauty that she didn't hear her friends calling her.

She also didn't hear an ominous sound.

Vroooom!

The pickup truck had started.

"Brisa?" Kona warned with a note of alarm in her voice. "I think they're leaving!"

Sumatra gazed at the long, hilly road that lead away from Leanna's farm.

"Leaving for who-knows-where!" she added.

"Tra, la, la," Brisa warbled.

Vroom, vroom!

The truck had shifted into gear.

"Brisa!" Sirocco, Kona, and Sumatra neighed together.

"*Hmmm?*" Brisa replied absently. She glanced up at her friends.

But before the three Wind Dancers could respond, the truck began driving off.

It gained speed as it turned out of the driveway.

It got even speedier as it drove down the first hill of the road.

But still, Brisa didn't take flight to rejoin the other Wind Dancers.

Her three friends gazed at each other for a moment. Instantly, they knew what they had to do.

"Fillies," Sirocco said, fluttering his wings and beginning to zip after the truck, "it's time to dash!"

. . .

Kona, Sumatra, and Sirocco had to fly like the wind to catch up to the pickup truck! When they did—hot and panting—the trio glared at the pink filly.

"Oh, hi!" Brisa chirped. "Isn't this fun? I'm so glad you came along on the ride!"

"*Ride?*" Sumatra sputtered. "You left us no choice *but* to follow you! And anyway, people don't pack this much stuff for a 'ride.' Leanna and her family are going on a major road trip!"

"And now we are, too," Kona scolded. She whinnied in alarm as the truck took a sharp turn.

"I have *no* idea where we are!" she announced.

"Silly!" Brisa giggled. "We're right here in Leanna's truck."

"And clearly that's where we're going to stay!" Sumatra said, her voice wobbling.

"Sounds like an adventure to me!" Brisa replied excitedly.

"I wonder where we're going," Sirocco chimed in, suddenly becoming excited, too.

Sumatra looked around the bed of the pickup truck.

"*Hmmm,*" she said. "We've got roses and a tomato."

"And don't forget Sara's pretty painted horses!" Brisa added, fluttering over to a box where the model horses were nested. "A pinto and an Arabian. They're so pretty! If only they had wings and comb-able manes and tails!"

As Brisa sighed over the missed beauty opportunity, Kona frowned in thought.

"Let's see," she mused. "Where would one

 16

take potted flowers, a giant tomato, *and*
painted model horses?"

But before Kona could figure it out, the
pickup truck began to slow down.

"Um, horses?" she asked, looking around.
"Wherever we're going, I think we're there!"

Craning their necks, the Wind Dancers
first saw a country road fence. The fence posts
were woven with small shrubby
plants dotted with dew-
drops that sparkled like
jewels. Beyond the fence,
the horses could see rows
of long, low buildings and
tents—and lots of excited
people.

They also spotted a giant Ferris wheel and
a twisty roller coaster.

They heard lots of laughter, applause, and
clanging bells.

They smelled popcorn, hot dogs, and doughnuts.

Finally, they gazed up at a giant banner. It read, "Welcome to the 44th Annual Fulton County Fair!"

CHAPTER 2
Pie in the Sky

"Oh, a fair!" Brisa cried in delight. "See? I *knew* this would be an adventure!"

Sumatra and Kona glanced at each other and stifled smiles. They knew their flighty friend hadn't had *any* idea where she was going when she'd perched in the truck.

"Well, since *you* brought us here," Kona said to Brisa, "you should decide what we do first!"

"*Ooh!*" Brisa replied. "I think we should ride the pretty Ferris wheel! Although, what's to stop us from flying up to the top ourselves?

19

So maybe we should follow Leanna and her beautiful big red tomato instead! I bet she's entering it in a 4-H contest. But then again . . ."

While Brisa went on, debating this or that activity, Kona noticed that Leanna's father was looking at his watch.

"Now remember, everyone," he was saying, "we have to be back on the road at three P.M. sharp so we can get home in time to milk the cows."

Kona pricked her ears up and looked at the sun. It was about nine in the morning.

"Whatever we do," Kona said, "we have to do it in the next six hours. We can't miss our ride back home!"

"Six whole hours!" Sumatra thrilled.

"Only six hours?" Brisa complained.

Kona laughed and looked at Sirocco.

"I guess this is what they mean when they

 20

say some see the glass as half empty," she said, "and some as half full."

"Forget half full!" Sirocco declared, his belly grumbling. "I need full-full! As in a full-full oatmeal milkshake. Or apple smoothie. Or carrot juice. If I don't get some grub soon, I'll collapse!"

"*Drama horse!*" Sumatra scoffed. But her growling stomach revealed that she was as hungry as Sirocco was.

All the foody smells in the air made it worse—for every horse except Brisa, of course. She was still deep in debate mode.

". . . I haven't even considered the quilt competition," she was saying. "Oh! I bet those quilts are so pretty. But what about—"

"—food!" Sirocco neighed, interrupting Brisa so loudly that she had to stop and pay attention. "What about *breakfast*!"

"Right!" Brisa said, without missing a beat. "That's a good idea. But where should we go? To the fast food tents on the midway? To the fruit and veggie displays? Or how about . . ."

Sirocco wasn't listening. Instead, he was sniffing the air. In one direction, he smelled the earthy aroma of just harvested vegetables. *Healthy!*

But when he turned toward a cheery striped tent and sniffed hot apples, cinnamon, and pastry, his nostrils flared. *Breakfast!*

"Let's go that way!" Sirocco whinnied. Without giving Brisa a chance to ponder any more, he dashed toward the tent. The fillies followed.

Inside the tent, a man was just stepping up to a microphone.

"Hope you're hungry, y'all!" he said. "The Fulton County Fair Apple Pie Eating Contest

will be startin' up soon! Now, you know the rules. Whoever can eat the most pies in ten minutes wins—you guessed it—more pies! And remember, no forks or hands allowed. This is a face-down-in-the-dessert contest."

The people milling about laughed, while Sirocco whinnied triumphantly.

"This contest was made for me!" he neighed. "After all, I don't *have* hands. And I am *very* hungry."

"We know, we know!" Sumatra said with a laugh. "An *eating* contest! Sirocco, I think you've found your dream event."

Kona laughed, too. Then she pointed to a wide metal beam that ran beneath the peak of the tent. It provided a perfect view of the pie-eating table—and looked like a comfortable place for four tiny flying horses to perch.

"There's a good place to camp out," Kona said. "We can keep an eye on the contestants below us—"

"—so you can tell that I've won!" Sirocco whinnied. "Now, we *just* need to find some pie for me."

"For *all* of us!" Sumatra replied hungrily.

"Sumatra and Brisa," Kona ordered, "you

 24

go look for apple pie. *I'll* prep our contestant for the big moment!"

She turned to Sirocco.

"Okay, we'll start with some simple jaw-stretching exercises," she began, "then move on to belly-poofing drills."

As Sirocco began stretching his mouth ridiculously wide, Brisa giggled, waved good-bye to her friends, and flew off.

As she fluttered above the tables, she admired all the pretty pies waiting to be  devoured in the competition. She had *every* intention of scavenging for forgotten pie bits for the fillies' breakfast and Sirocco's contest. But then, something else caught her attention.

In the next tent over was another set of tables groaning with food.

With *cakes*!

Lovely cakes. Four-layer wonders dotted with pink flowers. Coconut-dusted snowballs. Sheet cakes glossed with chocolate glaze.

"*Oooh!*" Brisa whinnied. Before she knew it, she'd left the pies behind for the creamy beauty of all those cakes!

Brisa was so enchanted that she did a happy little twirl in the air. And *that's* when she spotted the jelly jars on the other side of the cake tent.

The jars—which were filled with blueberry, blackberry, and strawberry jams—seemed to glow from within. Their colors were almost as pretty as those in Brisa's jewels!

The pink filly just *had* to take a closer look.

She flitted from one gleaming jam jar to the next, *ooh*ing and *aah*ing at the intense colors. She was even more enchanted when she realized that she could see her reflection in their glass!

At first, Brisa sighed at her own loveliness. But when she took a closer look at herself in a strawberry jar, she gasped.

Her pale pink coat was still pink, but no longer pale. In fact, she was bright red!

"I have a sunburn!" Brisa neighed. "Oh, no! How could I have let this happen?"

With scary images of red blotches rushing through her mind, she took flight again.

"Let's see," Brisa muttered to herself desperately. "What do you put on a sunburn? Lotion? Aloe vera? Butter? Or, how about butter*cream*!"

Brisa whizzed back to the cakes. She found the most luxurious-looking one—and swiped a big, soothing gob of frosting off it with her hoof. She dipped her head down to smear the icing all over her face.

"*Ahh,*" she sighed. "That's much better. Except . . ."

Brisa blinked—and felt her long lashes stick to her cheeks.

". . . except now I'm all sticky!" she neighed. "*Ohhhhhh!* What do I do now?"

The answer was clear, of course. Kona and Sumatra would get her out of this fix.

Brisa flew back to her friends. Only when she landed in their midst, above the pie-eating table, did she remember her original mission. She was supposed to have brought back some apple pie bits for all of them to feast on!

But there were so many other things to do and see, Brisa protested silently. *And there was also my dreadful sunburn to consider. Injured horses can't fetch pie!*

Luckily for the Wind Dancers, Sumatra had scrounged up a forgotten apple tart. Even after the fillies helped themselves to some apples inside it for their breakfast, it was still plenty big for Sirocco.

"I am *so* winning this contest!" the colt crowed.

"Yay for you!" Brisa said to Sirocco feebly, before turning to Kona and Sumatra.

"Look at me!" she neighed desperately. "I'm a bright red, cake-smeared mess!"

"Mess, yes!" Sumatra said through a nibble of sliced apples. "Red? Only if you're blushing because you ditched us!"

"I didn't mean to!" Brisa whinnied. "It's just, there were so many wonderful things to see. Cakes as tall as barns. And beautiful jellies. It was in a jar of strawberry jam that I spotted my horrible sunburn!"

"Um, Brisa," Kona said, gazing at the filly over her apple filling. "Did you just say *strawberry* jam? Maybe *that's* the red you were seeing. Because you're perfectly pink!"

"What?" Brisa twisted her head to look down at her belly and then at her flank. Kona was right. She was as unburnt and beautiful as ever!

"Oh, goodie!" Brisa burbled. "But I'm still sticky. Do you have a towel?"

Sumatra swooped down to the floor, nipped up a crumpled napkin, and tossed it to Brisa—just as the announcer grabbed the microphone again.

"Eaters, take your places at your pie plates!" he called.

"Here we go!" Sirocco whinnied, trotting

over to the apple tart and licking his lips.

"*Rah, rah,*" Brisa muttered vaguely. She carefully wiped her face with the old napkin, wishing it was a pretty, plush towel instead.

"Get ready, get set," the announcer yelled. "*Eat!*"

Sirocco dove into his apple tart.

Chomp. Gobble. Slurp. "Oh, yum!" he groaned. Then he *chomped, gobbled, slurped* some more.

"That's it!" Kona neighed to the colt. "Pooch out that belly, just like we practiced! Work those choppers!"

"Wow, Sirocco!" Sumatra cheered. "You're going to eat the whole thing!"

"Go, Sirocco," Brisa mumbled distractedly. Finally, she was satisfied that she'd returned to her original beauty.

"*Now,*" she said, "I can cheer Sirocco on proper—

Ding!

Sirocco stopped chewing and fell over. His face was smeared with apple filling. His belly was round and taut. And his apple tart was almost finished!

"That's it, y'all!" the announcer said. "And it looks like the winner is . . . big ol' Hugh Hartley, who consumed six entire apple pies! Hugh, you've won yourself a whole mess of more pies to take home!"

"But if you look at the size of that man compared to six pies," Kona rushed to assure the groaning Sirocco, "and the size of *you* compared to *your* tart, *you* clearly won. Your apple tart must have weighed *half* as much as you do!"

"Ohhhhh," Sirocco moaned. "I'm so full, I can't possibly eat ever again! Or at least until lunch."

"That's too bad!" Sumatra said with a gleam in her eyes. "Because here's your prize!"

She trotted to another crumpled napkin resting on the beam near the horses' perch and whipped it away. Beneath the drape was another discarded apple tart!

"I guess I could try to get another one down," Sirocco decided.

"Oh, do!" Brisa said eagerly. "I missed most of the contest, Sirocco, but I'm ready to watch you gorge yourself now!"

"No way!" Kona ordered the colt, as he unhinged his jaws to take a bite of his prize pie. "Sirocco, if you eat any more, you'll burst! Take that tart with you. You can have it later."

"Good idea!" Sirocco replied with a grin.

"Oh," Brisa added in disappointment. She hung her head. Sirocco may have been full to bursting, but *she* felt vaguely empty.

As the Wind Dancers fluttered out of the pie tent, Sumatra said to her friends, "What's next?"

Brisa felt hope bubble up within her again.

What's next? she wondered. *I don't know, but I hope it's something fabulous!*

CHAPTER 3

Show (Me the) Jump

As the Wind Dancers left the pie tent behind, Sirocco flew low and slow. (He was, after all, very full of pie.)

Sumatra skimmed beneath the clouds.

Kona bobbed along on a breeze.

But Brisa flew in a frantic zigzag.

"Should we go giggle at the dried-apple dolls," she wondered aloud, "or drop in on the painted-model-horse classes?"

When her friends didn't immediately answer, Brisa babbled on.

"There are weird chickens we could go

36

see," she added,
pointing with her
nose at a live-
stock barn. "Or
we could try out the
roller coaster!"

"Brisa reminds *me* of a roller coaster!"
Sumatra muttered to Kona. "She's all over the
place!"

Kona was about to laugh, but then she
spotted something that made her nicker with
interest instead.

"Look everyone!" she declared. "Look at
the big horses!"

The Wind Dancers followed Kona's gaze
down to several riding rings filled with horses
of all shapes and shades. They were trotting,
jumping, and cantering.

"*Ooh!*" Brisa neighed. "Maybe the big
horses can tell us what we should do next!"

"Brisa," Sumatra snorted. "The big horses *are* what to do next!"

"Oh!" Brisa said. "Are you *sure*?"

In answer, the other Wind Dancers simply swooped down toward the riding ring.

"Well, okay," Brisa said hesitantly. With one last longing look at the rest of the fair, she joined her friends.

Big horses leapt over the red-and-white-striped hurdles in one area, while others gaited past tables filled with judges.

Kona was drawn to one particular mare trotting with precise steps in a practice area outside one of the rings. She made a beeline for the mare, and the rest of the Wind Dancers followed.

"Hi, there!" Kona said. "We're the Wind Dancers."

"Oh, hello, little one!" the horse replied. Her whinny was throaty and she spoke

with a musical English accent. "My name's
Gemma."

"Oh, what do you do?" Brisa breathed,
fluttering up next to Kona.

"Well, today I'm an English pleasure ride,"
Gemma said proudly. "But I can also do
hunter under saddle!"

"Wow!" Kona said. "I'm not sure what
any of that means, but it sounds wonderful."

"I can show you, if you like," Gemma
said. "My performance doesn't start for a
while. I'll just run through our routine."

Gemma gestured with her white-striped
nose at her rider. Her girl wore a black fitted

jacket, a crisp white blouse with a stock tie at the throat, tan breeches, high black boots, and a helmet with a button on top.

"*Ooh,*" Brisa breathed, "*great* outfit!"

"Well, yes," Gemma agreed. "But getting a blue ribbon is about more than the rider looking nice in the saddle! It's about having smooth gaits, not mouthing your bit, and taking directions well. In short, it's my job to be a *pleasure* to ride!"

"Oh!" Brisa replied, delightedly. "And it's *my* job to be beautiful. Which is sort of the same thing, don't you think?"

Before Gemma could say more than "Not quite," Kona interrupted.

"Gemma?" she asked shyly. "English pleasure looks right up my alley. I mean, I'm all about making life *pleasant* for my friends."

"Yeah, her apple muffins are *awesome,*" Sirocco piped up.

 40

"Oh, can I try, too?" Brisa asked. "It'll only take me a moment to do my mane and tail and polish up my magic jewels."

She pointed an admiring nose at Gemma's trimmed tail, braided mane, and shiny bridle.

Gemma didn't seem to hear Brisa. She launched right into Kona's lesson.

"The trick is to control every part of your body, see?" she said, standing still and proud. "No tail-switching. No head-swinging. No tap-dancing."

Kona imitated Gemma's proud stance perfectly.

"Very nice!" Sumatra said enthusiastically from the sidelines, while Sirocco tapped his hoof on the ground in applause.

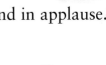

"What else, Gemma?" Kona said eagerly.

Brisa *tried* to pay attention. But her gaze wandered to the Hanoverians leaping over candy-striped poles and rectangular ponds in the show-jumping ring.

"They're so dashing!" Brisa whispered to herself. She drifted over for a closer look.

Before Brisa knew it, Gemma and her stately pleasure-class instruction had flown out of her mind. And she herself was flying over the red-and-white rails and water jumps along with the big show jumpers.

"*Whee!*" Brisa neighed to her fellow jumpers. "What fun!"

Before the huffing, puffing big horses could agree, Brisa glanced at the *next* riding ring over and gasped. That arena was full of horses even more dressed up than Gemma! They wore big, ornate saddles and colorful saddle blankets. Their riders wore ten-gallon

cowboy hats, fancy cowboy boots, and fringed chaps.

"This I've *got* to see!" Brisa whinnied. Leaving the show jumpers behind, Brisa darted over to the Western pleasure class area and began introducing herself.

"Ooh, I just *love* your Texas twang," she said to a quarter horse with an orange saddle blanket. But before he could say, "Thanky!" Brisa had flitted over to an Appaloosa.

"Howdy!" she said. "What's that step you're doing?"

The Appaloosa began to explain the fine art of loping, but before he could go into detail, Brisa had moved onto a pretty bay Morgan mare.

"However did you get such a lovely color?" Brisa asked breathlessly.

"Well," the Morgan chuckled, "it's not like I really had anything to do with that—"

But Brisa interrupted this horse as well.

 44

Gazing beyond the lovely Morgan, Brisa saw something that made her gasp!

"*What* is going on over *there?*" she breathed.

The mare followed Brisa's gaze to a ring of humans just outside the riding ring. The people, mostly girls, sat on camp chairs or blankets and balanced large notebooks on their knees. Standing in the center of this circle was a gorgeous Tobiano Paint filly.

The Tobiano was a glossy dark brown splashed with dramatic patches of white.

But the Morgan mare snorted with disdain at the painted filly.

"Oh, *that* Toby?" she said, using the nickname for the Tobiano color pattern. "She's a model horse. I mean, she's not a model of a horse, but a horse that is a model!"

"A *model*?" Brisa said with fascination.

"Yes, she's demonstrating horse anatomy for the 4-H class," the Morgan said with a sniff. "She doesn't jump hurdles or race. She's not a show horse either. She simply . . . stands still."

"Oh, but she does much more than that!" Brisa protested. "She stands still and looks *beautiful*!"

"I suppose," the Morgan said sounding bored.

Brisa was anything but!

CHAPTER 4
A Model Horse

Saying a quick good-bye to the mare, Brisa zipped over to the Tobiano and introduced herself.

"Hello, I'm Brisa," she said. "As you can see, I'm terribly gorgeous, just like you!"

The Toby's liquid brown eyes shifted slightly to glance at Brisa.

"So you are," the filly whispered through clenched teeth. "But there's only room for one beautifully turned-out horse in this class, little one. So if you wouldn't mind . . ."

"Oh, don't worry!" Brisa said wistfully.

She gazed with longing at the circle of sitting girls—many of them about Leanna's age. They were all studying the Toby and taking notes in their notebooks. "I'm invisible to humans!"

"Oh, well, then I suppose you can stay," the Toby answered again. "It's nice to have company, actually. Some of the other horses at the fair are a little standoffish. I think they're jealous! I guess that's the price one pays for incredible shape and form—otherwise known as conformation. Well, *you* know."

"Oh yes, it can be *hard* to be so amazingly perfect!" Brisa agreed, though she couldn't help grinning and feeling more than a little pleased about it.

"But isn't it satisfying to be able to show off your ideal self?" Brisa continued, fluttering next to the filly. "Everyone's *riveted* by you.

You're making them happy just by *existing*!"

"You *do* have a point." The Toby preened.

"I only wish I had your *job*!" Brisa replied. "Look how well *I'm* formed!"

Landing in the soft dirt next to the Toby's polished black hooves, Brisa stood with her head held high and her tail arched.

A moment later, she tired of that pose and dipped her head coyly, bending one foreleg.

"Then again," Brisa said, suddenly having a brainstorm, "*this* would make an especially great way to show off my shape." She fluttered into the air and stretched out her legs so that she looked like she was frozen in mid-leap.

"Or," Brisa mused, "how about . . ."

"Listen, fidgety filly," the Toby blurted. "There's no point in being so well turned-out if you don't hold still long enough for anyone to admire you!"

But before Brisa could consider this idea, she heard a voice on the loudspeaker. The announcer was calling all English pleasure horses to their riding ring!

"*Oops!*" Brisa neighed. "I think my show is about to start. Good-bye, my pretty!"

"And to you, my flighty friend," the Toby said, rolling her eyes.

·   ·   ·

As Brisa flew back toward Gemma and Kona, she fretted. "I was so busy being pretty in my perfect form, I didn't get to gussy myself up for Gemma's competition!"

Brisa landed next to Kona and immediately began popping jewels out of her magic halo and into her mane. She was so focused on her

hairdressing that she only listened with one ear to Gemma's final instructions.

"Just remember," Gemma advised, "always respond to your rider's orders. And do so pleasantly, of course!"

"Okay!" Kona agreed with a smile. "I think I've got the walking, the trotting, and the cantering down."

Brisa looked up from her beautifying.

"Um, can we go through that one more time?" she asked.

But Gemma's ears had already cocked forward. Her eyes sparkled with anticipation.

"The judge just signaled!" she announced. "We're up!"

"I'm right behind you!" Kona whinnied excitedly, wishing she was visible to humans so the judge could see her performance. Still, she was ready to put her all into it. Even the magic flowers in her halo stood at attention.

"And I'm right behind, er, you, Kona!" Brisa told the violet filly. Brisa gave her mane a gentle shake to make sure all her jewels were in place.

I'll just follow Gemma and Kona as they go, she told herself. *And I'll look fabulous doing it!*

As Gemma began her routine, Kona imitated her steps exactly. Kona's walk was as smooth as melted butter.

Brisa's was halting and hesitant because she didn't know how many steps to take.

Kona's trot *clop-clop-clopp*ed with perfect rhythm.

Brisa's trot was about as rhythmic as a broken drum.

Kona and Gemma turned first to the right,

 52

and then to the left.

Brisa went left, then right.

And when it came to cantering at just the right speed?

Brisa fluttered her wings and darted upward. Then she began trotting, cantering, and turning in the air, her magic jewels clinking together chaotically.

"Brisa," Kona muttered between clenched teeth. "What are you doing up there?"

"Improvising," Brisa chirped with a giggle. "If the judges could see me now, don't you think they'd love it?"

It was Gemma who answered—but not before she'd come to a neat stop in front of the judges' table and then trotted cleanly out of the riding ring.

"I'm afraid that the judges would have

disqualified you, Brisa," she said kindly. "After all, flying is *not* a legal part of the competition."

"Oh!" Brisa said. Then she grinned. "But don't I score points for my lovely mane and tail grooming?"

"I'm afraid not, darling," Gemma said. "The judges don't put style over substance."

"Oh!" Brisa said again. She hung her head as Gemma turned to Kona.

"But you, my dear!" she said. "You were brilliant! In fact . . ."

 Gemma trotted over to her rider's tack bag near the fence and nosed around inside it. She emerged with a first place ribbon that she'd won in another competition. She nipped a bit of the blue satin out of it.

". . . you deserve a blue ribbon!"
Kona gasped at the honor.

"I completely agree!" Sumatra burbled. She helped Kona tuck the tiny ribbon into her flowery halo necklace.

"Yeah! Bravo!" Sirocco added, clicking his hooves and grinning at Kona.

"Oh, no!" Brisa murmured to herself. "Why didn't I stick around and listen to Gemma's instructions? I could have had a blue ribbon, too! Of course, then I would have missed the show jumping. And the Western pleasure horses. And . . . come to think of it, if I keep on moping, I'll miss even more of the fair!"

So, while Gemma, Sumatra, and Sirocco continued to congratulate Kona on her performance, Brisa fluttered high into the air.

She gazed this way and that, searching for the next fare to sample at the fair.

That's when she spotted something in the distance.

Something that made her eyes go wide.

What was it? The most *gorgeous* horses ever! Lavender, pink, and robin's egg blue.

And they're not trotting, cantering, or galloping, Brisa thought. *They're flying!*

Brisa flew down to her friends and said: "You'll never guess what we're going to do next!"

"Have somebody guess how much we weigh?" Sirocco asked mischievously.

"No!" Brisa burst out with a grin. "We're going to meet some *other Wind Dancers*!"

CHAPTER 5

The Horses at the Fair
Go Round and Round

Brisa's friends followed her gaze. And just like her, they spied—

"Horses!" Sirocco neighed. "Brisa's right. Those *are* candy-colored horses just like us!"

"There's not a brown, black, or white coat among them!" Kona agreed.

"And they're definitely flying," Brisa said with satisfaction (and a sly glance at Kona).

"But where are their wings?" Sumatra wondered, squinting at the faraway Wind Dancers. "I can't see them."

"Well, you can't see them from all the way over here!" Brisa scoffed. "We need to get closer."

With an excited whinny, Brisa began flying toward the colorful horses, with her friends on her tail.

As the foursome got closer to the *other* Wind Dancers, the distant horses began to look bigger.

Much bigger.

"Wait a minute!" Sumatra said. "Those horses aren't tiny like us. There are *people* riding them! They look almost as huge as Gemma and all our big horse friends back home."

"Goody!" Brisa cried. "That means there's more of their beauty to enjoy."

"Wait *another* minute," Kona blurted. "If there are people riding those Wind Dancers, that means they're not invisible!"

"And look!" Sirocco observed as the tiny horses flew closer still. "They *don't* have wings!"

"Maybe they're not magic," Sumatra replied, confusion in her voice.

"But they're flying!" Brisa protested. "So maybe they're even *more* magic than us. You'd have to be to fly without wings, don't you think?"

Her friends couldn't deny that the beautiful, glossy horses were indeed flying. They floated one after another in a perfect circle beneath a round, light-filled canopy that looked like a spinning top. They seemed

59

to be dancing to some pretty music.

Finally, the Wind Dancers arrived at their destination, just as the big, colorful horses drifted slowly to a stop. All the children who'd been riding them clambered down, only to be replaced by a new bunch of laughing, happy riders.

And through it all, the big, pretty-colored horses never moved a muscle.

Sirocco gasped as he realized that each horse was attached to a tall, brass pole!

Sumatra's face fell as she noted that the horses were absolutely still. Their legs were stuck in mid-gallop; their heads frozen in mid-toss.

Kona went so far as to fly up to one horse's expressionless face. She tapped the creature's nose with one hoof.

Thunk, thunk, thunk.

"It's made of wood!" Kona neighed.

"*Awww,*" Sirocco sighed disappointedly.

"I had a feeling these 'Wind Dancers' were too good to be true," Sumatra complained.

And what did Brisa have to say about all this?

"Hello! My name's Brisa. It's so nice to meet you!"

Brisa hadn't heard a *word* her friends had said! Instead, she'd whizzed around the carousel and found the prettiest horse of all. (It happened to be coral-pink with a blonde mane.)

And now Brisa was blinking expectantly, waiting for the wooden horse to answer her!

"*Um,* Brisa?" Kona called gently.

But Brisa wasn't listening. She was too busy pricking her pretty ears at the fake horse, waiting for a response.

Of course, no response came.

"Oh, I understand," Brisa said to the wooden horse sweetly. "You're feeling shy. That's okay! I'll talk to some of your friends and come back."

Sumatra and Sirocco gaped at each other and tried not to laugh. Meanwhile, Brisa

 62

fluttered over to an ice blue horse, who gave her the cold shoulder.

From there, Brisa tried to introduce herself to yet *another* wooden horse. It, of course, ignored her as well!

Sumatra flicked her tail in agitation.

"How long do we have to wait before Brisa realizes that these horses *aren't* really Wind Dancers?!"

Chimey, chimey, chime . . .

Sumatra was interrupted by the carousel music. It was cranking up for another ride. The children sitting astride the wooden horses laughed with excitement.

Sirocco laughed, too. Then he flew around the merry-go-round. When he found a riderless wooden horse, he plunked himself down in its shiny saddle.

"Let's not just wait for Brisa to get wise," he declared to Sumatra and Kona. "Let's ride the ride!"

Kona grinned, nodded, and plunked herself down on a horse nearby.

A moment later, their horses began floating forward, as well as up and down!

"*Whoo hoo!*" Sirocco whooped while Kona whinnied in agreement.

Not wanting to miss the fun, Sumatra found a horse on the carousel's outer rim. Around her wooden horse went. Around, and around, and *around*!

"Well this is *sort* of fun," Sumatra murmured. But when you're accustomed to doing loop-de-loops among the clouds, tooling around in a circle can get a little old fast.

 64

Then, Sumatra noticed something!

Many of the children riding on the merry-go-round were standing up in their stirrups. They were making a grab for a wooden arm hovering above the spinning carousel.

Something seemed to be sticking out of the arm's end, but Sumatra couldn't tell what it was—until a little girl on a nearby horse snagged it.

"*Yay!*" the child cried, waving her prize in the air. It was a small, bright red plastic ring.

"Oh! It's not a brass ring," the girl complained to herself as she inspected her prize. "That's the grand prize! Oh well, I'll try for that the next go-round."

A brass ring? Sumatra thought. *How neat!*

Suddenly, this carousel ride seemed more exciting.

The next time Sumatra's wooden horse looped past the wooden arm, she lunged out for it. But she missed the arm by a long shot.

"Where's the brass ring? Where's the brass ring?" several of the laughing children called.

Where indeed? Sumatra wondered. *The ride's going to end soon and I* really *want to snag the grand prize!*

Sumatra hung her head. The ribbons in her magic halo sagged, too. One of them hung so low, it tickled Sumatra's nose.

Sumatra eyed her ribbon for a moment, then neighed exultantly.

"I know how to get myself a ring!" she cried.

Using her magic, she whipped up a super-long ribbon from her ribbony halo.

Then at *just* the right moment, Sumatra whipped her ribbon outward.

It coiled through the air.

It twirled around the wooden arm.

And on its way back to Sumatra, the

 66

ribbon hooked a ring and brought it back to her!

Whinnying in triumph, Sumatra looked at her prize. She saw it was a pretty *brass* ring. Sumatra had hit the jackpot!

CHAPTER 6
Eye on the Prize

Sumatra poked her head through her prize brass ring so it fit like a necklace. Then she fluttered over to Kona and Sirocco on their carousel horses.

"Look what I won!" the sea-green filly neighed.

"We saw!" Kona replied proudly.

"Yeah, that was awesome!" Sirocco added.

"Now we all have a prize!" Sumatra said, pointing to Kona's blue ribbon and Sirocco's apple tart.

"Well," Kona said with a cringe, "*almost*

 68

all of us. But not quite."

The three Wind Dancers gazed out of the merry-go-round and quickly spotted Brisa. She was perched on the roof of a nearby tent, looking despondent. When they flew over to her, the pink filly looked up at them sadly.

"Did you know," she said soothingly, "those 'other Wind Dancers' aren't Wind Dancers after all? They're not even real!"

"We know," Kona said. "But it doesn't really matter, does it? We had so much fun on the merry-go-round anyway."

"Fun?" Brisa muttered.

"It was fun for Kona, Sirocco, and me," Sumatra said. "We rode the wooden horses, just like the children."

"We were all laughing and yelling!" Sirocco added.

"Speaking of," Kona warned, squinting into the sky, "we better blast back to Leanna's pickup truck. The sun is looking awfully slanty, and we can't miss our ride home."

"Home!" Brisa cried as she followed her friends into the air. "But what about going to the funhouse? Or seeing the diving pigs? We also didn't get to taste the funnel cakes or hear a concert. And *I* didn't get a chance to win a prize!"

Sirocco, Sumatra, and Kona looked at each other guiltily as they flew toward the parking lot, toting their 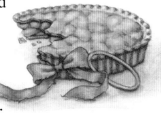 apple tart, brass ring, and blue ribbon.

"Well," Kona said, "instead of thinking about what we *didn't* do, let's think about what we *did* do. I mean, I didn't get to see the biggest pumpkin in the county, but I *did* get to learn how to be an English pleasure horse. I'll never forget that—or Gemma."

 70

Sumatra fluttered her wings happily.

"And *I'll* always remember the merry-go-round," she said. "With the help of my brass ring!"

"I almost ate my weight in apple pie!" Sirocco joined in. "So what if I didn't get to gorge myself on funnel cakes, too!"

"Now *you* tell us," Kona prompted Brisa as they flew along. "Of all the things you did at the fair, what will you remember most?"

Brisa frowned and thought hard. But instead of being able to focus on only one wonderful thing, her memories were a blur.

Just like her entire day.

Brisa hung her head as she and her friends reached the bed of Leanna's truck. They were followed almost immediately by Leanna and her family.

"We timed it just right!" Kona said proudly. "Now we'll be able to make our way home."

Brisa nodded, but gazed wistfully back at the fair.

"If only I could do it all over again," she whispered to herself regretfully. "I would have *done* less and *enjoyed* more!"

She perked up, though, when Leanna and her family loaded their things into the truck bed. Leanna's tomato box had a fluffy red ribbon pinned on it, and one of Sara's painted horses wore a white ribbon that read,

"Honorable Mention." Their mother's rose bush was ribbonless, but she didn't seem to mind.

"I can't believe I had the *second* biggest tomato at the fair!" Leanna was saying. "I guess all that weeding and watering was worth it!"

"I'm glad I won, too," Sara said, holding her painted horses. "I only wish I'd also had one of those red velvet cupcakes we saw."

"Me, too!" Sirocco piped up with a grin.

As the fillies gaped at him, Leanna said, "There's always next year!"

"Next year?" Brisa said. "Next year?"

She whirled around to face her friends.

"We can come back *next* year?"

"Definitely!" Sirocco said.

"When we come back," Kona added sweetly, "you can enjoy things that you missed today."

"Yay!" Brisa neighed. She fluttered over to

Leanna's mother's rose bush and gave one of the blooms a sniff.

"Next year," she said, "maybe I'll spend all day in just the flower exhibit alone!"

"Wow, that's really stopping to smell the roses!" Sumatra said, her eyes twinkling.

"Right," Brisa said happily. "I'll check out the supersized sunflowers and the prize peonies. And I wouldn't want to miss the cut-flower arrangements and the perfume-making demonstrations! And—"

Kona, Sumatra, and Sirocco smiled and rolled their eyes as Brisa chattered on.

"That's our Brisa!" Kona laughed, flying  over to give the still-chattering pink filly a nose nuzzle. "And," she added, "we love her just the way she is!"

You Say Tomato . . .

As the Wind Dancers flew over the dandelion meadow the next night, Sumatra's brass ring glinted in the light of the setting sun.

The blue ribbon around Kona's neck rustled in the breeze.

Sirocco's muzzle was dusted with crumbs from his prize dessert of apple tart.

And Brisa was still without her own prize.

But she was far from sad about it. Because she was free to carry something else!

Slung around her neck was a loop of ribbon (made from Sumatra's halo) sized to fit a child's wrist. And dangling from this bracelet was a single ruby-red jewel charm.

The charm was round and sparkly. It was in the shape of a tomato! One that would last long after Leanna's real prize-winning tomato was gone.

When the Wind Dancers arrived at the farmhouse, Brisa whizzed through Leanna's bedroom window.

The girl was fast asleep. On the night-stand, next to her bed, a small diary lay open. Brisa couldn't help but read the latest entry.

The county fair yesterday was the best! Not only did my tomato win second place, thank you very much, but I got to watch some show horses jumping. I bet the Wind Dancers

 76

would have loved *it!*

Brisa's ears perked up. Even at the fair, Leanna had been thinking of them!

"We were thinking of you, too," Brisa whispered. "We always are!"

To prove it, the tiny filly shimmied the charm bracelet off her neck. She gently laid it on Leanna's pillow, along with a note she'd scratched out herself on a piece of bark:

After your "charmed" day at the fair, here's one perfect memory to keep and treasure. Come next year, we'll add another!

Before she rejoined her friends, Brisa hovered above the sleeping girl. She smiled down at her with all the fondness in her heart, and whispered, "I'll always have my memories of yesterday, too. See you again soon, Leanna!"

Here's a sneak preview of Wind Dancers Book 11:

Horsey Trails

CHAPTER 1
Fly Away Home

One bright summer morning, as they flew across the dandelion meadow, the tiny Wind Dancers were especially bubbly.

Being near the girl who had brought the Wind Dancers to life with one puff on a dandelion always made the magical little horses happy. Today was no different—until the four friends landed on the windowsill of Leanna's room.

And their faces fell.

"What—what's this?" Brisa gasped.

"A big mess is what it is!" Sirocco exclaimed. Normally, Sirocco liked all things messy, but he knew Leanna, and she was a neat-as-a-freshly-combed-mane sort of girl. So he knew that *something* was up!

"There are shorts and T-shirts and riding breeches everywhere!" Sumatra agreed. "And what are all those tubes and bottles?"

Kona flew in for a closer look.

"Shampoo, sunscreen, bug spray, and a travel-size tube of toothpaste," she reported.

The Wind Dancers also spotted a small, pink diary and stationary with stamped, addressed envelopes.

And all of this stuff was piled around a big, army-green duffel bag.

"Leanna's going away!" Brisa exclaimed.

"Where to?" Sumatra gasped.

Before the horses could speculate, Leanna herself tromped into the room with her little sister, Sara, on her heels. "Help me out, won't you?" she said. "Mom wrote my name in most of my clothes already, but there are a few extra things I have to pack before tomorrow. *Everything* has to be labeled!"

"Why should I help you," Sara said, jutting out her lower lip, "when you're about to leave me for a week at horse camp? It's no fair!"

The Wind Dancers gasped, then gazed at each other.

"Horse camp!" Brisa breathed.

"Wait a minute," Sumatra gasped. "A sleepaway camp with horses? That's like a dream come true!"

"Especially for Leanna. She thinks horses are the best!" Sirocco crowed. "Because we are, of course!"

The Wind Dancers exchanged excited looks.

Then suddenly, an idea occurred to Sumatra.

BREYER
Wind Dancers
Continue the Magical Adventures

Musical Jewelry Box

Journal

Trinket Boxes
Collect All 4!

Sirocco
Sirocco
Brisa
Sumba
Kona

Memory Book

Find these and other Breyer models, activity sets and more at your favorite toy store!
Visit us online at **www.BreyerHorses.com** to get a free poster* and to register for online newsletters!

©Reeves International, Inc.

*While supplies last